This book belongs to

_____

"God's gifts of grace come in many forms.
Each of you has received a gift in order to serve others.
You should use it faithfully."

1 Peter 4:10

© 2006 Big Idea, Inc.

VEGGIETALES®, character names, likenesses, and other indicia
are trademarks of Big Idea, Inc. All rights reserved.

All scripture quotations, unless otherwise indicated, are taken from the
HOLY BIBLE, NEW INTERNATIONAL READER'S VERSION®. Copyright © 1995,
1996, 1998 by International Bible Society. Used by permission of Zondervan.
All rights reserved.

Published by Scholastic Inc., 90 Old Sherman Turnpike, Danbury, Connecticut 06816.

This product is available for distribution only through the direct-to-home market.

ISBN: 0-7172-9842-6

Printed in the U.S.A.

First Scholastic printing, February 2006

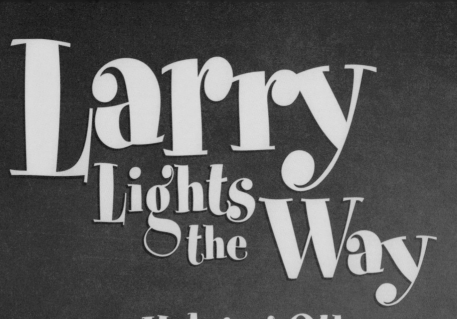

Larry
Lights
the Way

A Lesson in Helping Others

written by
Mary Murray

Illustrated by
Big Idea Design

SCHOLASTIC INC.

New York Toronto London Auckland Sydney
Mexico City New Delhi Hong Kong Buenos Aires

In a faraway land lived a king who was special. He knew he was special because God made him, and everything God makes is special. One of the talents God gave him was being very good with a pogo stick. Because King Nezzer was quite frightened of drawbridges, he used his pogo stick talent to jump right over the moat. That way he never had to worry about using the drawbridge again!

Nebby K. Nezzer was a good king. He knew God wanted him to serve his people in good times and in bad. He even enjoyed teaching others his favorite pogo sport. He especially liked teaching his royal assistant, Archie, and his cousin, the young prince who would become the next king. Prince Junior loved taking pogo stick lessons from King Nezzer. In turn, Junior shared with the king his talent of making up riddles. Together, they both had a wonderful time.

But the king no longer teaches pogo stick lessons or listens to Junior's riddles—not anymore—because one day, a traveling salesman came to visit. He insisted that pogo sticks were no longer very special. "A king like yourself needs a unicycle. All the best kings ride them." So King Nezzer tried the unicycle. But he couldn't get his balance! He couldn't figure out how to work the pedals!

Worst of all, he couldn't use the unicycle to jump over the moat! That made him very cranky. It made King Nezzer so cranky, that he forgot he was special. He no longer cared about leading the people, and he no longer cared about his pogo stick. Nebby K. Nezzer became a very grumpy king.

The king became quick to criticize and complain. He rarely said a kind word to anyone. "Gourds—stop wobbling!" he would bellow to the guards. "And no tossing rings to the ducks in the moat today!" Then he would leave for his morning walk, fearfully hop over the drawbridge, and shout, "It's too noisy in the village square!" The sounds of singing, laughter, and storytelling quickly came to a halt. "And get rid of all that color!" he would grumble as he passed by the pretty paintings displayed by the villagers.

No one was cheerful anymore, except for Larry the Lamp Lighter. He was a very joyful cucumber. "Isn't that a beautiful sunset?" Larry would ask as he went about his job. Or, "It sure is fun to help others by lighting up their night!"

One day, King Nezzer came down with the chicken pox and was no longer able to perform his kingly duties. So eight-year-old Prince Junior was anointed and took over this great honor. King Junior knew that God had made him special, so he wanted to be a very special king. He began his first day in the royal palace with a bowl of Fruity-Os for breakfast and challenged his royal assistant, Archie, with a riddle. But then he realized that kings should do things that are more kingly! So he walked through his new kingdom to meet the people.

He quickly noticed that everyone was grumpy. The people complained!
The people pouted! The people grumbled!

"I must do something about all this grumpiness," said the new king.
"I can't let this go on." Then he met Larry the Lamp Lighter.

"Good day, King Junior," Larry said cheerfully. "I hope you enjoy
your new job as king."

"Thank you, Larry the Lamp Lighter," replied the king, quite surprised
by Larry's cheerfulness.

Later that day, King Junior sneaked away

to his royal tree fort to spend some time alone. "I wonder what God thinks about grumpiness. I don't think he wants people acting like this—no one is happy!" he thought aloud.

Just then, the king spotted Larry outside the castle lighting the lamps. He watched as Larry whistled, smiled, and lit each one. "Hello, Royal Guards. You're looking swell today," Larry said cheerfully. He seemed quite happy.

The king wondered what made Larry different.

When Archie called King Junior for his royal snack, the king told him about the grumpy people and then about Larry. "Why do you think he is so different from the other villagers?"

Archie thought for a moment. "Maybe it's because Larry likes to use his own special abilities to help others."

"Of course!" said King Junior. "God gave each of us different abilities. He made everyone special in some way."

"You're good at telling riddles, and I'm good at taking care of you," Archie continued. "Wasted talents would certainly make one grumpy, because God made us to help others in our own special way!"

"Maybe if the people start using their talents to help one another, it will make everyone feel better, and they won't be so grumpy. I know just what I'm going to do!" King Junior said.

The king called all the villagers together. When everyone had gathered, he made the following proclamation: "Hear ye! Hear ye! The villagers in this kingdom have been grumpy long enough!

I have a riddle for you to solve, and it goes like this:

God made you special; he loves you a lot!

So what should you do with the talents you've got?"

Then the king explained, "You have one week to figure out the riddle.

Then each of you will present your answer at a royal banquet."

"What?" "Huh?" "What does he mean?" The people in the village began to fret. Never before had a king given a riddle to solve! They didn't know what to do. Soon the people became grumpier than ever!

The news about the king's riddle and the grumpy people spread throughout the land. So when a traveling salesman heard the news, he thought he would come to town and help. He decided to fill his cart with happy-wares. So he loaded it down with yellow smiley-face pins, funny hats, and comic books.

"Come and get it!" he shouted. "I've got everything you need to stop being grumpy. Guaranteed to get rid of the grumps or your money back."

When the village people saw the cart of happy-wares, they remembered that the king wanted them to stop being grumpy. "Hey! Maybe this stuff will help us solve the riddle," the people said. "It looks like an easy way to get rid of grumpiness." So the people bought everything that the salesman had.

Everyone in the village wore the smiley-face pins, put on the funny hats, and read the comic books. The people smiled. The people laughed! But their happiness did not last long.

"This can't be the answer to the king's riddle. Look at us. We're grumpy again," they complained.

"Maybe that's because happiness doesn't come from buying happy-wares," Perciville Pea suggested.

"Then what does it come from?" they asked.

Larry the Lamp Lighter watched as the people tried to figure out the king's riddle. "I wish the people could see how special they are," he said to himself. "Then they'd be happy on the inside."

So Larry set out to encourage the villagers. When he came upon Madame Blueberry, she was looking rather blue. "Good morning, Madame Blueberry. What's wrong?"

"I don't know what to do. Boo hoo hoo hoo. I can't solve the king's riddle, and the banquet is only three days away," she cried.

"Remember when you sang that beautiful song at my birthday party two years ago?" Larry asked her.

"Why, yes. I remember that well," she said with a sparkle in her eye.

"Why don't you use the talent you've got to sing at the royal banquet? It might cheer everyone up," Larry suggested.

"What a wonderful idea! Thank you, Larry," she said with a smile.

Madame Blueberry was so encouraged by what Larry had said, that
she shared some encouragement with her blueberry friends.
Together they formed a blueberry choir!

Larry continued through the village and saw Sir Lunt sitting in his workshop, grumping about what to do. "Sir Lunt, you're good at building things. Why don't you use your talent to build something special for the village?" suggested Larry.

"Hey, you're right! I am good at building things! I could build something for everybody! Why didn't I think of that? Thanks Larry," he said. "I'll try it."

Larry also helped Jean Claude by reminding him that he was good at sculpting macaroni. He encouraged Laura, who loved to read stories and talk on the phone, to consider sharing her talents as the town storyteller. And he encouraged the royal guards to use their ring-tossing abilities to become lifeguards at the town pool.

"Look at us!" exclaimed Laura. "We're each good at something different."

"You're right!" agreed Sir Lunt.

"And we're happy helping others," Madame Blueberry added.

"It looks like we have solved the king's riddle!" the people cheered.

The night of the royal banquet

finally arrived. Sir Lunt presented a model of a new playground for the village children. Laura told a story called "Goldilocks and the Three Pears." Madame Blueberry sang a song about being thankful, and announced that the blueberry choir would be performing at the village park every Wednesday evening. Jean Claude shared a variety of sculptures he made to display at the town square. And the guards demonstrated how their ring-tossing talent could be used at the village pool. Best of all, they all performed their talents with a smile, because they were happy on the inside.

And Nebby K. Nezzer watched the entire event from his bedroom window in the upper chambers of the castle.

King Junior was pleased. He knew the people were happy,
because they were using their talents to help others. He
praised the people for solving the riddle.

"But wait," said the king. "What about Larry? He hasn't presented anything yet."

"Well, sir, lighting lamps is about all I'm good at. And the sun is setting, so I'd better head out to do my work," Larry told them cheerfully.

At that moment Madame Blueberry stepped forward and bowed before the king. "Your Highness, there is something else that Larry's good at doing—encouraging others! He showed me that God made me special by giving me a talent for singing. He helped the others by encouraging them to use their talents, too. Larry the Lamp Lighter has shed light on the villagers in a new way. He's helped light the way to happiness in our hearts."

"She's right!" declared the king. "Larry, you have helped to light the way for the others. You have encouraged the whole village."

"Hip, hip, hooray!" the people shouted as they lifted Larry high into the air. "Larry lights the way!"

Larry was invited to sit with the king at the royal banquet. During the meal Larry continued to encourage the king. "Hey, nice milk mustache," he joked. And then, "You know, you're a pretty good king."

King Junior wiped off his mustache. "Thanks, Larry. Do you want to play in my royal tree fort after the banquet?"

"Perhaps I can teach Larry how to work a pogo stick," said Nebby K. Nezzer as he hopped out from his royal bedroom.

It seems that King Nezzer was feeling better. He'd heard all about how Larry had reminded the villagers that God made them special.

So Nebby K. Nezzer went back to being king. He also went back to teaching others pogo stick lessons. After all, that's how God made HIM special. And in the village, where everyone used their talents to help others, grumpiness went away. Now happiness ruled the day—thanks to Larry, who helped to light the way.

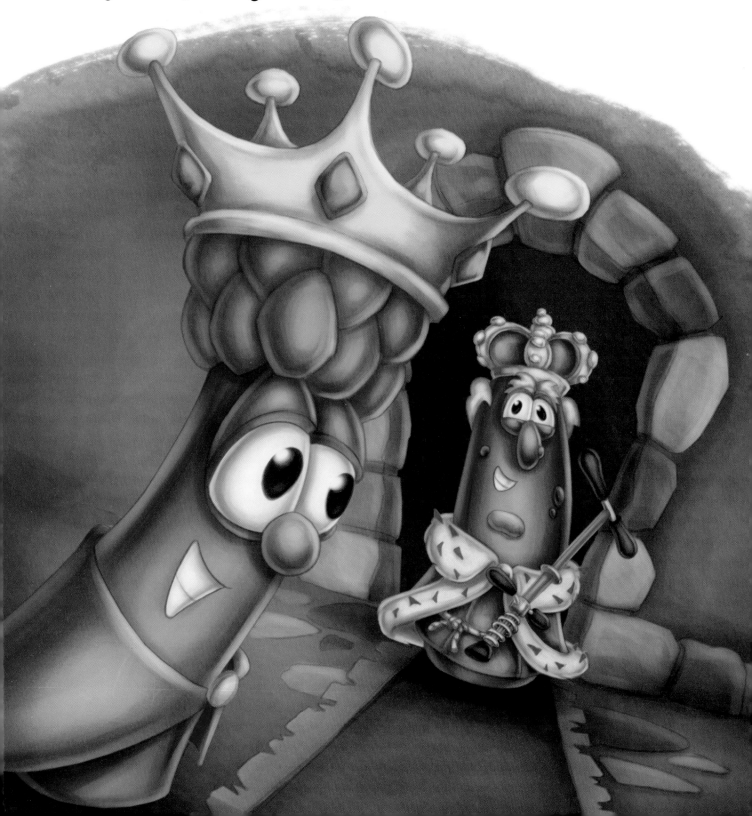

EYE SPY

Hip, hip, hooray!
Larry lights the way.
Can you find these
pictures in the story?

Veggie Value to Share

In this story, Larry reminds the villagers that God gave everyone different abilities and talents. In what ways did God make you and your family members special?